MW00916399

Here's what some young mystery readers
are saying about *Chase For Home*:

"Reifman combines nail-biting suspense with
great detail to create an amazing plot."
—Kirun Cheung

"I couldn't put the book down. I really admire
how Chase stands up for himself."
—Sara Cooper

"A perfect book for both boys and girls of all ages."
—Jenny Kean

"This book made me think hard."
—Ace McAfee

CHASE

For Home

CHASE

For Home

Chase Manning Mystery #2

STEVE REIFMAN

All rights reserved. No part of this book may be used or
reproduced in any manner without written permission except
in the case of brief quotations embodied in critical articles or reviews.

Copyright © 2014 Steve Reifman
All rights reserved.

ISBN: 1500784400
ISBN 13: 9781500784409

To Mom, Dad, Lynn,
Jeff, Sylvia, Alan, Ari, and Jordy.

To all the family, friends, teachers,
and students whose support, expertise, and encour-
agement made this book possible.

Table of Contents

Acknowledgments xi

Chapter 1: 8:30 a.m. 1

Chapter 2: 8:56 a.m 9

Chapter 3: 9:03 a.m 15

Chapter 4: 9:09 a.m 21

Chapter 5: 9:19 a.m 25

Chapter 6: 10:05 a.m 29

Chapter 7: 10:13 a.m 33

Chapter 8: 10:56 a.m 39

Chapter 9: 11:09 a.m 43

Chapter 10: 11:15 a.m 45

Chapter 11: 11:32 a.m 51

Chapter 12: 11:49 a.m 57

Chapter 13:12:08 p.m 65

Chapter 14: 12:17 p.m 69

Chapter 15: 12:46 p.m 75

Chapter 16: 12:55 p.m 79

Chapter 17: 1:02 p.m 85

Chapter 18: 1:11 p.m 91

Chapter 19: 1:51 p.m 97

Chapter 20: 2:16 p.m 103

Chapter 21: 2:23 p.m 107

Chapter 22: 2:31 p.m. 113

Chapter 23: 2:40 p.m. 117

Chapter 24: 2:47 p.m. 121

Epilogue. 129

About the Author .133

ACKNOWLEDGMENTS

I would like to acknowledge the wonderful work done by the entire CreateSpace team. You are all true professionals. It has been a genuine pleasure working with you.

I would also like to thank Amy Betz for her fantastic editing and Lorie DeWorken for her awesome cover design.

Tuesday, May 11th

CHAPTER 1

8:30 a.m.

Fever hit Apple Valley Elementary twice in the late spring. The first wave came out of nowhere and spread quickly. Unlike most outbreaks, however, which led to aches and pains, this one created excitement and joy. That's because this fever wasn't caused by any germ or virus, but by the surprisingly red-hot Apple Valley baseball team. The squad was only two wins away from its first league championship, and nobody could believe what was happening. In the past, football had always been king at Apple Valley. Not anymore. Baseball Fever was sweeping the entire town.

"I finally got my wish," Coach Turner said, giving me a wink from the side of the stage as the other classes began entering the auditorium.

"What wish is that?" his assistant asked.

"Twelve years. I've been at this school for *twelve years*. I've coached championship football teams, championship basketball teams, and championship track teams. Not once has there been an assembly honoring one of my teams, until today."

As I listened, I thought I saw a smile appear on Coach Turner's face. Of course, I couldn't be sure about this because I hadn't ever seen this expression and had nothing to compare it to. A smile on Coach's face was something else the school had never experienced before.

What Coach Turner didn't mention was that it wasn't so much his great coaching that led his team to this point. Not to brag, but it was actually the clutch hitting of Apple Valley's newest and most unlikely baseball star, me.

After finding the missing cello and saving the school's music program nearly seven weeks ago, I felt proud of myself, and my confidence grew. Baseball had never really been my thing, but I was on a roll and thought the time was right to try something new. So, I joined the baseball team.

There was only one problem—I stunk at baseball. "Hey, guys, check out 'The Fan' over there," one of my teammates had yelled from the infield during my first batting practice. "He may not be able to hit the ball, but he swings hard and makes a nice breeze for everyone in the immediate area.

Having Chase Manning on your team is like having your own private air conditioner." Very funny.

All that changed one night at home when I sat down to talk about my hitting with my grandfather, Woody. I had always thought people called him Woody because it was short for Woodrow, but recently I learned that he used to be a star baseball player and had earned the nickname because he was such a strong hitter with his wooden bat.

"Chase," Grandpa had said, "it wasn't so much the bat that made me a great hitter. It was the lucky batting glove I wore at the plate." Then he pulled the glove out of a carved wooden chest and declared, "This is yours now. I hope it brings you as much luck as it did me." Since then I've kinda been on fire, producing one game-winning hit after another and leading my team into today's semifinal game against our cross-town rival Walnut Grove and its legendary slugger, Jason Roberts.

I'm not normally that competitive, but I have to admit my teammates and I had come down with a serious case of baseball fever and wanted to win today's game badly. The cool thing is that everyone at school knew how important I'd become to the baseball team, and everyone knew about my lucky new batting glove. It had become famous.

At first, it was only my teammates who made a big deal about the glove. Some of them touched it before the start of every game. A few even talked to it. Coach Turner got into the act when he gave the glove its own seat on the bus when we drove to away games. I thought that was a bit much. Then things really got out of hand when a bunch of fans in the stands started holding up signs with a picture of my good luck charm and a caption that read: "We glove you so much."

As well as things had been going lately for the team, today's game was sure to be a tough one. Based on everything I've heard, Jason Roberts was simply the best young baseball player the state had ever produced.

"A-choo!" sneezed Jenny Gordon, my classmate and close friend. The two of us were sitting next to each other on the floor with the rest of our class as the assembly was set to begin. Jenny looked like she was about to ask me something, but then it happened again. "A-choo!"

"Are you OK?" I asked.

"I'm fine," she replied. "It's just a couple sneezes. A-choo. A-choo."

"You sure?"

"Yes."

I was a little concerned about Jenny because I knew that Baseball Fever wasn't the only thing in the air at this time. The last few weeks had also brought Spring Fever to Apple Valley, the worst flu epidemic to hit the area in decades. More kids than ever had been absent from school, and I couldn't recall seeing so many empty seats during an assembly.

As I looked to my right, I noticed that Jessica Kingman, Apple Valley's newest student, was in perfect health. In fact, Jessica was all smiles, and I knew why. She was looking forward to two events today: the tomato showing preview that her Gardening Angels club would give at 2:45 p.m. and PE class, where Coach Turner had promised her she could pitch the entire game for her softball team. I heard her talking to Jenny about both things the whole time we were walking down the hall to the auditorium.

On the stage Coach Turner grabbed the microphone and invited all the members of the baseball team to come up and join him. A few moments later we all lined up from one side of the stage to the other, and Coach introduced each of us individually. After saying the first few names, Coach continued.

"I'd now like to announce our next player, Brock Fuller." As the hot-tempered sixth grader stepped forward, he expected to get the loudest cheers of all, but he actually got the quietest. Brock didn't take this too well. He turned his hands into fists, started growling, and quickly shot to the front of the stage staring everyone down. All the kids in the audience panicked and started to cheer as loudly as they could. Brock's growl turned into a proud smile, and he went back to his place in line.

After introducing several more players, Coach was ready to say the last name. "Our final player is Chase Manning." I was shocked by how loud the cheers were for me. Brock growled and shot me a look.

"A-choo!" went Jenny again.

Jessica Kingman pretty much cheered for every player the same. The one person she didn't seem to support was me. I wasn't surprised.

On the day Jessica arrived at Apple Valley right after spring break, she told me what a big deal she had been at her old school. "I was always the center of attention," she had said. "The very center. I'm sure it will be the same way here. I starred in all the plays, had tons of friends, and impressed my teachers with my excellent work. Always excellent. The spotlight was usually on me, and I loved life in the spotlight. Absolutely loved it."

Around that time, the spotlight was on me because I had just found the cello, and now it was on me again because I was hitting so well for the baseball team. Jessica seemed to be trying harder and harder to get people to focus on her, but it wasn't working.

After introducing the team, the Coach tried to get the crowd even more excited about today's game by jumping around the stage and screaming at the top of his lungs. The whole scene reminded me of a bad cheerleading movie I once saw on television after one of the detective shows I liked to watch. When Coach was done, he pulled himself together, held the microphone up to his face, and said one last thing.

"I have one more announcement to make. I know many of you are looking forward to PE today."

Instantly, a look of concern appeared on Jessica's face, and she seemed to be worrying that Coach might make a change and take away her chance to pitch.

"I have a change to make about PE."

"Uh, oh," Jessica groaned.

"I just wanted to let you know," the Coach continued, "that I have arranged it so that PE class will be extra long today."

"Yes!" Jessica cried out. "Today is definitely going to be my day."

8:55 a.m.

CHAPTER 2

8:56 a.m.

"Just who does that woman think she is?" PTA President Alice Simmons grumbled as she stormed out of the school office.

Across the hallway, the assembly was now over, and all the classes were exiting the auditorium. A whole bunch of kids looked Alice's way when they heard her outburst. I was one of them.

"Hi, Mom, what's wrong?" asked her daughter Amy.

"Oh, hello, sweetheart," Alice replied. "It's just this whole business with our garden."

When they saw Alice and Amy talking about the garden, the rest of the Gardening Angels approached and joined the conversation. The club had eight members, seven girls and one boy—school bully, Dave Morrison.

Poor behavior had kept Dave out of the orchestra, off the baseball team, and away from every other club at Apple Valley. Mrs. Simmons, the leader of the Gardening Angels, felt sorry for Dave and invited him to join Amy, Jenny, Jessica, and the rest of the girls. He accepted the offer and has been with the group ever since. Nobody knows for sure, though, whether he even likes gardening or whether he just likes being part of a club. Sometimes, he seems embarrassed about being the only boy in the group, but Mrs. Simmons tells him over and over again how gardening is a great activity for both boys and girls and how wonderful it is for him to be part of the Angels.

"Mom, what woman were you talking about a minute ago?" Amy asked.

"Ms. Fletcher," Alice responded. "She sent me an e-mail yesterday saying there was nothing she could do to help us with our garden situation. What nerve! So, I just went to her office to discuss the matter with her, and she wasn't even there! She thinks she can say *no* to me? We'll just see about that!"

Patty Fletcher, Apple Valley's Assistant Principal, had recently taken over for Tom Andrews as school principal after the police arrested the former boss for stealing the valuable cello that was donated to the school to save its music program. Ms. Fletcher would remain principal until the school's hiring committee found a permanent replacement.

As for Mr. Andrews, he would be spending the next two years of his life in jail. To make matters worse, he wasn't going to just any jail; he would be serving his time at Manning State Prison, a building 20 miles away that was named after a former governor. No relation. And as if all this wasn't bad enough, his job during this time was to answer the phone in the main office. Every time it rang, he would have to say, "Hello, Manning State Prison. How can I help you?"

Each time he said the name *Manning*, I imagined it would serve as yet another reminder of the fifth grader who helped put him there.

Before the whole mess involving the cello, all the school principals got together to finalize the event calendar for the rest of the year. That schedule did not do the Gardening Angels any favors.

If my baseball team won its semifinal game this afternoon at Walnut Grove, the school would host the championship game next Wednesday. The Annual Tomato Showing was scheduled for next Thursday, a day after the baseball game. At the showing, judges would come and inspect everything the Gardening Angels had grown over the past couple months. After visiting the gardens of all the other schools, the judges would announce the winner. As badly as my teammates and I wanted to win the baseball championship, Alice Simmons and her Angels wanted to win the Tomato Showing.

The problem for the Gardening Angels was that championship games are big community events in Apple Valley, and people from all over the area come to watch. That meant the school would need to put in more bleachers, a snack bar, and a place for all the television and newspaper reporters to work. To make room for everything, Mr. Andrews decided that if our baseball team made it to the championship game, the tomato garden would have to be flattened.

At the time of the decision, nobody was too concerned about this possibility. After all, an Apple Valley baseball team had never made it to the championship game before, and there was no reason to believe that we would make it that far this year. Now, it was a different story. Of course, if my team lost today, our school wouldn't be in the championship game, and the garden could stay.

I'd heard Jenny talking with the other Gardening Angels about this situation for the past few days, and they were in a panic. Some of the girls were beginning to panic right now. Mrs. Simmons noticed their faces and tried to comfort everyone.

"You girls, and Dave, have worked too hard and come too close to the showing for our garden to be destroyed now," she told them.

The rest of my class had left the area by this point, and I was supposed to be with them, but I couldn't tear myself away from Alice's conversation with the club. I knelt to the ground and pretended to tie my shoelaces to make it look like I had a good reason for sticking around. Even though I knew I shouldn't, I always smiled when she made an announcement to the Angels as if they were all girls and then suddenly remembered to mention Dave. This had happened many times.

Alice continued. "You girls, and Dave, have nothing to worry about. I will take care of everything."

Again, I smiled and even started to laugh a little bit. I couldn't help it. I hoped Dave didn't notice, but when I looked up, he was glaring right at me. Instantly, I turned away and started looking at Alice.

"Let me say one last time," Alice announced, with her angry eyes meeting mine, "I make you one promise. I will not let this situation rest."

9:02 a.m.

CHAPTER 3

9:03 a.m.

Despite their leader's proclamation, the members of the Gardening Angels were still visibly upset as they walked back to their classes. It was easy to understand why. They had spent a lot of time growing tomatoes for next week's showing, and I'm sure the last thing they wanted was for their garden to be destroyed because of some baseball game.

The only one in a good mood was Jessica Kingman, who cheered herself up by talking to nobody in particular about all the pitching she was going to get to do during this morning's lengthened PE class. "I've never pitched before, and I absolutely can't wait for the game to start. Can-not wait."

Jessica was certainly dressed for the occasion. She had on a baseball cap and matching jersey, but her outfit didn't stop there.

"Why is she wearing that big baseball jacket?" Jenny asked me.

"Her father told her that professional pitchers wear jackets like that to keep their arms warm," I replied.

"Is that really necessary today?"

Jenny had a point. It did seem silly for Jessica to be wearing that jacket now. After all, she was only going to be throwing underhanded, not overhanded the way the pros do, not to mention the fact that it was already seventy-four degrees outside.

While Jenny and I were talking, Jessica moved next to Amy Simmons and started telling her about all the different pitches she was going to throw during the game. She had been talking non-stop about these pitches since yesterday.

"I'm going to use my fastball," she bragged, "then my curveball, then my change-up." I didn't know if Jessica had any idea how to throw these pitches, but she sure talked as if she could. Jessica was a good talker.

When she was done describing her pitches, Jessica remarked that even if she weren't pitching today, at least softball was a nice break from what the class had been doing lately for PE—tag games. "I absolutely *detest* tag games. De-test them. My least favorite *by far* is Doctor Tag. Can-not stand Doctor Tag."

In Doctor Tag the coach chooses three or four kids to be the taggers and a few others to be the doctors. The taggers run around trying to tag everybody. If you are tagged, you have to freeze and kneel down. You can only get back in the game when one of the doctors comes around and gives you a pretend shot.

"This game brings back terrible memories for me," Jessica added. "Just ter-ri-ble. When I was younger, I had some bad experiences getting shots. Very bad experiences. In fact, I would rather go to the dentist than play Doctor Tag. I swear, I would. I honestly would."

"A-choo! A-choo!" Speaking of doctors, Jenny looked as if she might need one soon. Her coughing and sneezing were getting worse.

Dave Morrison walked back to class by himself. He looked angry. I couldn't tell whether Dave was mad because of the garden situation or because he had seen me laughing earlier. There was one thing I did know; Dave stared at me the whole way back.

Just as the upper grade classes were almost back to their rooms, Wendy Marshall came up to me. Wendy was one of the nicest kids at school, and I had known her ever since her family moved down the street from us six years ago. Recently, Wendy's family moved to a different part of Apple Valley, and her cousin Ryan, a second grader, moved with his family into her old house.

Wendy didn't usually talk to me, and I wondered why she was approaching.

"Chase, I just wanted to tell you how great it is that you've become such a good hitter with your new batting glove," she said.

"Thanks."

"I mean, I can remember a few weeks ago when you couldn't hit anything."

I didn't know what to say to that.

Wendy continued, "I mean, you couldn't hit water if you fell out of a boat."

I definitely didn't know what to say to that.

"But I just wanted to tell you one more thing."

"What's that?"

"Even though you're pretty good now, you'll never be as good as my cousin."

I was confused. Ryan was only seven years old, and he didn't even play baseball.

"I'm sorry, Wendy, what did you say?"

Wendy repeated herself. "I said that you'll never be as good as my cousin."

I needed a break from this conversation, so I took a look back to see if Dave Morrison was still glaring at me.

He was.

9:08 a.m.

CHAPTER 4

9:09 a.m.

As my body entered the classroom, my brain was still thinking about Alice Simmons and the look she had on her face after the assembly. She told the Angels she wasn't going to let the situation with the garden rest. I was trying to figure out exactly what she meant by that when I heard the phone ring.

"Hello, student speaking," Jenny said a few seconds later.

"Mrs. Kennedy," she said, approaching the teacher after receiving the message, "that was the office. They want Chase to come get his lunch. It was just dropped off."

Mrs. Kennedy saw that I was listening to Jenny's message, and our eyes met.

"Should I go now?" I asked.

"Yes, but hustle," she quickly replied.

I popped up from my desk and hurried down to the office. When I made my way inside, a loud voice caught my attention.

"Knock, knock," Mrs. Simmons sang out. She seemed to be in a much better mood than she was earlier. I stuck close to the wall to hide myself from everyone in the office. I was pretty sure this conversation was going to be about the garden.

"Oh, hello, Mrs. Simmons," Ms. Fletcher replied.

"Why, hello, dear. I tried catching you earlier this morning, but you were out. So, I thought I'd try again. Do you have a minute to talk?"

"Well, I'm actually quite busy now, Mrs. Simmons. I just got back from a meeting and need to get some work done, but for you, sure, have a seat."

"Oh, thank you, dear, and please call me Alice."

"OK, Alice, what can I do for you?"

"Oh, no, it's what I can do for you, dear," Alice said in the most charming voice I'd ever heard.

"Thank you," Ms. Fletcher said.

"You look so nice today, dear. Is that a new suit? It's simply beautiful."

"Thank you."

"You know, I just wanted to tell you that as head of the hiring committee, I am so excited to consider your application to be Apple Valley's new principal. Why, I was telling the others yesterday what a fine choice I think you would make. I know it's been your lifelong dream to become a principal, and that dream may be only a few days away from coming true."

"Thank you, ma'am."

"I was also sharing with the others what great judgment I think you have, like with this unpleasant situation with the tomato garden and this, this baseball game," Alice said. "I'm sure you'll do the right thing."

"I'd love to help you and your club," Ms. Fletcher replied, "but as I said in my e-mail yesterday, as acting principal, I simply do not have the authority to change the schedule Mr. Andrews created."

"Don't even mention that thief's name to me!" Mrs. Simmons responded sharply.

"Sorry, Alice, I—"

"All I know is this," Alice interrupted, rising to her feet and getting louder. "It would be in your best interest to solve this scheduling problem to my satisfaction."

Alice's flattering words were suddenly turning into threats.

Ms. Fletcher didn't say a word.

Mrs. Simmons then sat back down and once again found her charming side.

"Sure," Alice continued, "if the baseball team loses today, then my garden would be safe and you wouldn't have to do anything else. But if they win, we'll see what kind of decision you make. And decision-making will be one of the main things my committee looks at when we hire our next principal."

Alice stood up, and it seemed as if she was about to leave the office, but she just stood there for a while. "It would be such a shame, dear," she added, "if a silly little baseball game kept you from getting the job of your dreams."

With that, Alice Simmons walked out of Ms. Fletcher's office. When I saw her coming, I left my spot on the wall and made a move toward the counter. She passed me without breaking stride. I retrieved my lunch and headed back to class. As I went by Ms. Fletcher's door, I heard her mumble something to herself.

"I need a way out of this mess."

9:18 a.m.

CHAPTER 5

9:19 a.m.

"Aaaa-choooo!"

Back in class, Jenny was on her last legs. I had been in the room for only a short time, and that was already her seventh sneeze.

My classmates and I were sitting quietly at our desks editing our Writing Workshop stories. For this stage of the writing process, Mrs. Kennedy had taught us to use a special four-color pen to correct the different kinds of mistakes we might find. We checked for run-on sentences with black, capitals with blue, commas and other punctuation with red, and spelling with green.

Mrs. Kennedy sat at her desk conducting one-on-one editing conferences. After finishing with one person, she looked up and smiled when she saw everyone hard at work.

"Jessica, may I see you for a moment?" my teacher called out.

"Sure, what about?"

"I want to talk to you about your writing," Mrs. Kennedy said as Jessica approached her desk and took a seat.

"Why, because it's so descriptive and creative?" the girl asked pompously.

"No, because it's so messy," Mrs. Kennedy responded firmly. "I don't understand why you can't write more neatly, like Chase. Look here. I have two writing samples. Here's yours. Here's his. Take a look at his writing. It's beautiful. Now let's take a look at yours. It's...it's...well, let's just say, his is beautiful. You should try to make your writing more like his."

Jessica nodded, but her face turned bright red when she realized that several kids were able to hear this whole conversation. I was one of them. She glared at me and stomped back to her seat.

A few minutes later Wendy Marshall stood up and passed me on her way to the back counter to grab a tissue. Very quietly, she whispered, "You know, Chase, my cousin is really a great baseball player."

I ignored her.

We continued to work well for the next few minutes, but one student started to have trouble focusing. Me. Out of nowhere I began to close my eyes and daydream about today's big game. I pictured myself up to bat in the last inning with the score tied.

Mrs. Kennedy noticed my daydreaming right away. "Chase, your baseball game isn't until this afternoon. Let's keep our minds on our writing."

Hearing Mrs. Kennedy scold me brought a big smile to Jessica's face. Right away Mrs. Kennedy noticed this, too.

"And Jessica, your tomato showing preview also isn't until this afternoon. Sitting there smiling all day isn't going to make your writing any neater. Let's keep our minds on our work."

Even though Mrs. Kennedy was the one snapping at her, Jessica turned her anger towards me. In her opinion, I was always the one keeping her from getting the attention she deserved. Her face turned even redder.

Mrs. Kennedy wanted to put a stop to this distraction once and for all. "Class, may I have your attention for a minute?" she asked. "I know many of you are looking forward to the big gardening and baseball events later today, but could we please all try to do a better job of keeping our minds on our work."

At the mere mention of the word *baseball*, Wendy blurted out, "Mrs. Kennedy, my cousin is really good at baseball. He's even better than Chase."

"That's wonderful, sweetheart. Now let's keep our minds on our writing."

Mrs. Kennedy's little talk to the class worked. Everyone did a good job of editing, and all was quiet until the end of the period when she asked us to put our papers away and get ready for PE.

Realizing it was time to go outside for her softball game, Jessica's spirits rose. When Mrs. Kennedy reminded everybody that PE would be even longer today, Jessica became even more excited.

"This is going to be the best PE period of my life," she muttered. "Of my life."

10:04 a.m.

CHAPTER 6

10:05 a.m.

The fifth and sixth grade classes gathered at the kickball diamond where we always met to begin PE. Brock Fuller was directly to my left, so I instinctively moved a few feet to my right. Though he and I were teammates now, being close to him still made me nervous, and I avoided him whenever possible.

Jessica Kingman was all business. She had her game face on and was ready to pitch. To warm up her throwing shoulder, she started windmilling her arm forward and then windmilling it backward. The dirt marks on the ground in front of her caught my eye, and I noticed she had changed out of her regular shoes and was now wearing cleats.

"I have an announcement to make before we start PE," Coach Turner bellowed.

His last announcement in the auditorium was great news for Jessica because it resulted in a longer PE period. She sat up taller and leaned forward with a look of eager anticipation on her face.

"As you know, I promised all of you there would be a special softball game today," the Coach said.

Jessica smiled.

"I also wanted PE to be extra long today."

Jessica started beaming.

Coach Turner went on. "Though I'm really not supposed to use our PE time to help my after-school teams, I need to make a change."

"Uh, oh," Jessica groaned.

"We have a big game today, and the reason I wanted a longer PE period was so that I could have one last practice with my baseball team before our semifinal game against Walnut Grove."

Jessica's jaw dropped to the ground.

"So," Coach Turner continued, "I am canceling the softball game and sending everyone who's not on the baseball team to the other side of the playground with my assistant. I'll be over on the field with my team."

Jessica was fuming.

"When the rest of you get to the other side of the playground, you will be playing a series of tag games."

Steam was practically coming out of her ears.

"The first game you will play is...Doctor Tag."

Jessica's face was now redder than the tomatoes she was growing over in the garden. Earlier, she said that she would rather go to the dentist than play Doctor Tag. One thing was certain. If she kept biting down in anger the way she was now, she would need to go to a dentist any minute.

Coach Turner then announced that Assistant Principal Patty Fletcher would be on the playground helping his assistant supervise the tag games. When the Coach introduced her, she had an unusual expression on her face. I wasn't quite sure what to make of it. It almost looked to me as if she was trying to figure something out in her head.

As everybody left the kickball diamond and moved to their PE spots, I saw Alice Simmons over by the newly installed gardening shed getting ready for this afternoon's tomato showing preview. She was sweating buckets working outside in this heat, and I was impressed by all the time she was putting into the gardening club.

She must really want to win this contest, I thought.

10:12 a.m.

CHAPTER 7

10:13 a.m.

Watching the other kids from the field, I could see that this was turning out to be the worst PE period of Jessica Kingman's life. After only a few minutes of action, she had already been tagged three times, received three shots, and yelled at three kids to get away from her and leave her alone.

To make things worse, even if she wanted to play Doctor Tag, which, of course, she didn't, wearing the cleats she was expecting to use for softball on the grass field made it incredibly difficult for her to run around on the hard playground, not to mention unsafe.

She was in complete misery.

Coach Turner was putting my teammates and I through a number of drills. Without a doubt the early star of practice was Brock Fuller. His speed around the bases was incredible. He may have broken his arm and index finger in a skateboarding accident several weeks back, but there was obviously nothing wrong with his legs.

Brock was by far Apple Valley's best athlete. He wasn't a particularly good student, and sports were his way of getting attention. On the field and on the court, Brock shined.

Two months ago, before our team played its first baseball game, Coach Turner had high hopes for the upcoming season, and he was counting on Brock to carry the team. According to the Coach, Brock Fuller was "The Man."

When the season started, Brock still hadn't gotten his cast off and couldn't play in the first couple games, both of which we lost. Coach Turner was frustrated. At that point, Brock Fuller wasn't "The Man," and I was still "The Fan." Our chances of making the playoffs seemed bleak.

Then, Grandpa gave me the lucky batting glove, and everything changed. My strong hitting led to four Apple Valley wins in a row and made everyone forget about calling me "The Fan." All of a sudden, I was becoming "The Man." It felt pretty good.

Sitting on the sidelines watching someone else get all the glory wasn't easy for Brock, and he complained about it all the time. It became especially difficult when he realized the new hero couldn't even hit the ball a few weeks earlier. On top of all that, Brock felt that Coach Turner blamed him for the team's two losses. Brock didn't think it was fair to be blamed when he had a cast on his arm and couldn't play, but Coach Turner had been hard on Brock all season.

Ever since Brock got his cast off and rejoined the team, he had been on a mission to outdo me and reclaim his role as the team's star. Sure, Brock wanted to win the league championship, but even more than that, he wanted once again to be "The Man."

Even though the morning was a hot one and we had a big game later, Coach Turner was working us hard. As he had done all season, he was encouraging to me and tough on Brock.

"Good job, Chase. Good hustle."

"Let's go, Brock. Pick it up. Can't you go any faster than that?"

After the base running drills, we practiced our fielding. Coach Turner stood at home plate hitting ground balls to all of us at our different positions. When Brock and I both dropped the first ball hit to us, his unequal treatment continued.

"Good try, Chase. Stay with it. You'll get it."

"Come on, Brock. Get in front of it. I didn't teach you to do it like that."

Brock didn't take these words too well. No matter how hard he tried and how well he played in the games, Coach Turner still talked to him this way.

Batting practice was the final part of the PE period. Brock and I were the last two players to take a turn hitting. Brock had one last chance to upstage me, and I could tell by the look in his eyes that he was determined to make the most of it.

On the first pitch Brock swung hard and nailed one that landed just over the fence separating the field from the teachers' parking lot, barely missing Coach Turner's car. As he ran around the bases, everyone cheered. Brock allowed himself a smile and carried himself as if he was "The Man" again.

I was next. I usually didn't hit with much power. Solid ground balls and line drives were more my game. In fact, every one of my game-winning hits had been a line drive over an infielder's head. I fouled the first few pitches away, but on the fourth pitch, I connected. My bat met the ball with a thundering crack that could be heard all over the playground. Never had my bat made a sound like that.

All the other kids stopped what they were doing and watched as the ball flew way over the fence and landed next to the wall on the opposite side of the parking lot.

Circling the bases, I couldn't believe how far I had just hit the ball. Nobody could. This was a great moment for me on one of those beautiful spring days where it feels great just to be outside. I took my time going around the bases, soaking up this awesome feeling and wanting to savor the experience for as long as possible.

I was on top of the world.

10:55 a.m.

CHAPTER 8

10:56 a.m.

"**H**uddle up," Coach Turner commanded at the close of practice. My teammates and I quickly dropped our gloves, bats, and other equipment and ran over to meet him on the far side of the field.

"I have some final announcements to make about today's game," he said. "First, the bus to Walnut Grove will leave right after school at 3:10. Don't be late."

Coach Turner then went on to tell our team what a tough opponent we'd be facing today.

"Guys, we'll need to be at our very best this afternoon. Walnut Grove is a great team, and that Roberts kid they got is the real deal. There's even a rumor he hit a ball over a building last week that hasn't landed yet."

"Yeah, Coach," our catcher said, "I saw him at the mall a few days ago. Are you sure that kid's only eleven? He's huge! I heard he already shaves—and drives!"

"Well, anyway," Coach replied, "if you ask me, someday he will be wearing a major league uniform. Why, he's even much better than our star hitter."

Brock smiled when he heard the words *star hitter*. Then, the Coach continued.

"As I was saying, he's even better than our star hitter, Chase."

Brock looked at me and growled.

The Coach wrapped up his little speech by talking about the season and about how far we had come as a team in such a short time.

"How did we do it?" Coach Turner asked.

None of us dared to speak up because we knew he was going to answer his own question. He always did.

"How did we do it? Well, there are many factors that explain how we overcame such a disappointing start to the season," he said looking at Brock, "and turned it around the way we did. Teamwork. Hustle. Great coaching, of course. But I'd have to say that we wouldn't be where we are today without the lucky batting glove and clutch hitting of Chase Manning."

All the other players cheered as Brock just sat there in anger.

Not counting Brock, spirits were high as we left the huddle and went to grab our equipment.

I was still so excited about hitting the longest home run of my life, I kept looking back and forth between home plate and the spot in the parking lot where the ball landed. I was the last person to gather my stuff and head back to class.

I picked up my mitt. I picked up my bat. I looked down one more time, but something wasn't right. After a few seconds, I realized that something was missing.

Then it hit me.

My batting glove was gone.

11:08 a.m.

CHAPTER 9

11:09 a.m.

For the second time in the past two months, I had discovered a major theft at Apple Valley Elementary. Seeing that my own batting glove had disappeared, however, gave me a far different feeling than the one I had when I noticed the cello was missing from its display case in the entryway to the school office.

Mr. Andrews had stolen the cello to get rid of Mrs. Washington and destroy Apple Valley's music program. That crime had hurt the whole school. Maybe someone took my batting glove to hurt the whole baseball team so we would lose today against Walnut Grove.

But I didn't think so.

My first instinct told me that somebody took my grandfather's glove not to harm the baseball team, but to harm *me*. In my mind this wasn't a crime against Apple Valley Elementary. It was a crime against Chase Manning.

The cello had belonged to the PTA, to the entire school community, really. The glove belonged only to me, and I felt violated.

The first crime made me feel angry.

This one felt personal.

More than anything else, though, I felt alone. Picking up my remaining equipment and heading back to class, I needed to talk to someone. I was stunned and confused. I had a bunch of questions, but no answers. I couldn't wait to get to the room and talk to Jenny about what had just happened.

She was helpful last time when I searched for the missing cello, and I was already counting on her to help me find my batting glove.

I needed Jenny now more than ever.

I entered the room and quickly looked around for my friend. When I didn't see her, I walked up to Mrs. Kennedy.

"Where's Jenny?" I asked.

Then, my teacher told me the bad news.

Jenny had just gone home sick.

11:14 a.m.

CHAPTER 10

11:15 a.m.

"**R**ing!"

"Chase, can you get that, please? Jenny's not here."

"OK, Mrs. Kennedy." I put down my silent reading book and hustled to the phone.

"Oh," my teacher suddenly remembered, "can you also take over for Jenny as Student of the Week for the rest of the day?"

"Sure."

Normally, I would have been excited about having an extra chance to do all the Student of the Week's jobs, but considering what had just happened with my glove, it didn't seem so important.

I really needed someone to talk to.

"Mrs. Kennedy, it's the office," I reported. "Mrs. Gonzales says it's extremely important and needs to speak with you."

"Can't she just leave a message? I'm very busy right now."

"I'll check," I said. After talking for a few seconds with the office manager, I returned to Mrs. Kennedy.

"No, she says it's super important, and she needs to speak directly to you."

"Oh, all right, all right," Mrs. Kennedy muttered as she got up from her chair. She didn't like being interrupted in the middle of class time.

I eavesdropped, but I could hear only bits and pieces of my teacher's conversation with Mrs. Gonzales.

"Uh, huh,...OK...Now?...OK...Send them down."

Mrs. Kennedy hung up the phone, walked to the front of the room, and signaled for everyone's attention. It turned out that Spring Fever had claimed another victim.

"Class, I wanted to tell you that Mrs. O'Connor, the fifth and sixth grade teacher from upstairs, has just gone home sick. Since the school day has already started, there's no time to find a substitute. Her class is going to be dispersed. That means her students will be sent in groups of four to the other upper grade classrooms. We can expect them to arrive any second now."

Suddenly, the whole room started buzzing with anticipation about which four of Mrs. O'Connor's kids would be coming to join us for the rest of the day. I think I was the most interested person of all. My spirits began to rise because I knew Amy Simmons was in Mrs. O'Connor's class, and I was hoping she was on her way downstairs that very minute. The two of us were friends, and even though I wasn't as close with Amy as I was with Jenny, I figured that with my friend Skip home sick today, she would be the best person to help me right now with my missing batting glove.

Soon, the door opened, and all eyes focused on the first two of Mrs. O'Connor's students to enter the room. One was a boy; the other, a girl. Both were sixth graders. I really didn't know them at all. I was getting nervous now, wondering if Amy would be one of the last two kids to come inside.

Dave Morrison arrived next. Unlike the first two visitors, Dave came empty-handed—no backpack, no lunch. I subtly checked to see if Dave was glaring at me, but, surprisingly, Dave just came in with his head down and quietly took an empty desk near the back of the room.

Three students down, one to go. Suspense was building over this final person's identity.

"Oh, *please* let it be Amy," I said to myself, practically begging at this point.

The fourth guest stormed in a second later, and it wasn't Amy Simmons.

It was Brock Fuller.

"Oh, no!" I said to myself, shaking my head in disappointment. Brock's arrival meant that Amy Simmons would not be spending the rest of the day in our class, and I would have to find the missing batting glove without the help of someone I truly trusted.

I put my head down on my desk with a thud, covered my ears with my hands, and shut my eyes to try to escape from this mess. I began to think that all hope was lost.

Unexpectedly, the door opened again, and a fifth student from Mrs. O'Connor's class entered the room.

I looked up and couldn't believe what I saw.

It was Amy Simmons.

"Yes!" I blurted out.

Everyone started staring at me.

Though I was confused by this turn of events, I decided not to waste any time asking how my class got a fifth student when it was promised only four. Instead, I took advantage of this pleasant surprise and invited Amy to sit next to me at Jenny's open desk.

Amy seemed happy to see me, but not half as glad as I was to see her. Immediately, I started to tell her about the missing glove.

"I have some bad news for you, and I'm hoping you can help me," I began.

"Chase, what happened? You look terrible."

"I feel terrible. At baseball practice someone took my batting glove."

"Seriously?" she replied.

"Yes."

"Are you sure it was stolen? Maybe you just misplaced it."

"I'm sure. I had it with me until the end of practice, and when I went to go get it after Coach talked to us, it was gone. I checked everywhere on the field, but I couldn't find it."

"Wow, that's awful. How can I help?"

"Do you think I should tell an adult, or do you think it's better if I try to solve this case myself? I'm thinking that I should probably tell Mrs. Kennedy. It—"

"Chase, you didn't need other adults to help you find the cello," Amy interrupted. "You spent the whole day tracking down the thief, and you found him. You found the cello, and you were the big hero. I do *not* think you should tell an adult about this crime yet. And keep this in mind. If the word somehow got out that your glove was stolen, the thief may get nervous and do something drastic. You're better off keeping this news to yourself and letting the thief get a sense of security. I definitely think you should solve this case by yourself."

I was impressed that Amy could come up with such logical ideas so quickly. I was beginning to change my mind and agree with her. After all, she did make some good points, and, I had to admit, it sure felt nice hearing her refer to me as "the big hero." Amy's words were building me up and boosting my confidence.

After thinking about everything a bit longer, I was ready with my decision.

"OK, we'll try it your way. I'll solve this case myself," I declared. Looking at Amy, I realized how lucky I was to have her there.

I appreciated having a friend around.

11:31 a.m.

CHAPTER 11

11:32 a.m.

Having just decided to try to find the missing batting glove without the help of an adult, I started to talk with Amy Simmons about possible suspects and their motives.

"I have a pretty strong feeling that I know who did this," Amy said.

"I think I do, too," I replied, hoping we had the same person in mind.

Amy went first. "I think it was Brock. He's been jealous of you ever since you got that glove and started winning all those games for the baseball team. Plus, while I was playing tag during PE, I looked over at the field a few times and saw him glaring right at you. He hates it that you're now the star of the team. It makes complete sense. He takes the glove, you stop hitting, and he becomes the star again."

Once again, I was impressed with Amy's quick thinking. Everything she said did, indeed, make sense, but I had someone else in mind.

"I think it was Jessica Kingman."

"Jessica? Why would you think she did it?" Amy asked, a bit upset that I would accuse a friend of hers.

"It's no secret that I'm not one of her favorite people," I said. "Ever since she came to this school, she has wanted to be the center of attention, and when it doesn't happen, she always seems to blame me for it. And this morning, before you got sent to our class, she was mad because Mrs. Kennedy said my work was better than hers."

Amy disagreed. "But that's not enough of a reason to think that Jessica—"

"There's more," I interrupted. "You know how much she was looking forward to pitching during the PE softball game today. Why, she even wore that big jacket—and cleats! When Coach Turner canceled the game and said there would be tag games instead, she was furious. She easily could have just snapped and grabbed my glove to punish me for all her problems."

"I still don't think Jessica did this," Amy protested.

"There's more," I repeated. "Jessica is also part of the Gardening Angels. She knows that if we win our game today, the school is going to level the garden. So, besides getting back at me, taking the batting glove also hurts our team and makes it more likely that the garden will survive for the tomato showing. I think that when you put all that together, she is clearly our number one suspect."

Amy didn't say a word.

There was an awkward pause between us, and I was trying to figure out why Amy was so quiet. After a minute, she spoke up.

"Chase, if you think Jessica could have taken your glove because of the situation with the tomato showing, then that means you think any of the Gardening Angels could have done it."

I didn't like where this conversation was going. "It's possible," I said gently.

"Then that means you think Jenny or I could have done this? Jenny went home sick. Do you think I could have done this, Chase? Do you think I took your batting glove?" she asked with a hurt look on her face.

I really didn't like where this conversation was going.

"No, Amy, I don't think you did it. I don't suspect you."

"But you did last time," she fired back, looking me right in the eye.

I suddenly understood why Amy had become quiet a moment ago and why she was getting a bit emotional now.

When I looked for the missing cello before spring break, Amy was one of the suspects Mr. Andrews had me investigate. I realized that the two of us hadn't yet had a chance to talk about everything and clear the air. I also sensed that Amy was still holding on to some hard feelings about being accused of something she didn't do.

Looking back, I realized that I had been so focused on finding the cello that when I determined she didn't do it, I simply forgot the whole thing and moved on. Apparently, Amy hadn't.

"Amy, I don't suspect you," I said, pausing and becoming a little emotional myself. "I made that mistake once, and it almost cost me two of my best friends."

We decided to leave it at that and turn our attention to finding the batting glove. I didn't want to go through any more drama and agreed to investigate Brock first, even though I still believed Jessica to be the thief. I was happy to put all this behind me.

"Let's get on with business," Amy said.

"OK, how are we going to investigate Brock?" I asked.

Amy's face lit up a minute later, and she proudly announced, "I have a plan."

Without telling me anything about her idea, Amy picked up a pencil and headed over to the sharpener in the back of the classroom. As she passed Brock's desk from behind, she dropped the pencil at his feet and kept walking. Brock had a huge crush on Amy, and she knew it.

Noticing the pencil on the ground, Brock picked it up and delivered it to Amy. When he returned the pencil, Amy acted as if that was the nicest thing anyone had ever done for her.

"Oh, thank you so much, baseball star," she said as she gave him a hug. She held on to the hug for a few seconds so she could look down to see if the glove was in any of his pockets.

No luck.

Amy's hug made Brock blush so much that he ran up to Mrs. Kennedy's desk and asked to use the restroom. Mrs. Kennedy was busy meeting with another student and had no idea what had just happened or that Brock liked Amy. The teacher let him go and went back to her meeting.

"And now for part two of my plan," a beaming Amy said to me.

"What?" I replied. "You mean you knew all along he would ask to leave class?"

"Yep."

I was beginning to realize that Amy could be just as clever as Jenny.

With Brock out of the room, Amy moved quickly. She first checked the inside of the desk where he was sitting, but no luck.

The batting glove wasn't there.

Next, she hustled to the closet, found Brock's backpack, and looked around to make sure nobody was watching her. She checked all the zipped pockets as quickly as she could.

Still no luck.

There was no sign of the batting glove anywhere. Amy managed to put everything back in the closet and return to her seat just before Brock walked in the door.

Hmm, I thought, *I wonder if he could have hidden the glove somewhere else.*

11:48 a.m.

CHAPTER 12

11:49 a.m.

Whether or not Brock Fuller could be ruled out as the thief at this point, I realized there wasn't anything more Amy and I could do to investigate him now.

I was eager to turn my attention to my number one suspect, Jessica Kingman.

"OK, Amy," I whispered. "Now we can move on to Jessica. Let's figure out how we're going to investigate her."

"Wait!" said Amy. "I've been thinking about it, and there's someone else we should investigate first."

"Who's that?" I asked, puzzled.

"Dave Morrison."

"Dave? More than Jessica? Why do you think that?" I asked, even more puzzled.

"Actually," Amy explained, "for many of the same reasons I suspected Brock. Dave has also been very jealous of you. Look, you found the cello—and got to keep it, for goodness sake! Because of his bad behavior, he can't even be in the orchestra next year. Now, you're this big baseball star, and he wasn't allowed to join this team, either. He wasn't allowed to join any club until my mom let him in the Gardening Angels. He comes to all our meetings, but none of us know if he even likes gardening."

I wasn't convinced. As I sat there quietly, Amy decided to push her case further.

"Come on, Chase," she continued, "you can't tell me that you never suspected Dave. I'm sure you've noticed how he's been acting lately."

"Actually," I admitted, "he did see me laughing earlier this morning in the hallway when your mom kept forgetting to include him as one of the Gardening Angels."

"See? Anything else?"

"And he was glaring at me when we were walking up the hall after the assembly," I said, beginning to see Amy's point. "Maybe you're right."

"Of course, I'm right," she bragged. "Let's investigate him next."

"I'm still not sure, Amy."

"I have one more reason to suspect Dave," Amy said, not backing down. "When the five of us came downstairs after

Mrs. O'Connor went home sick, we all brought our back-packs, except Dave."

"Maybe he doesn't have one, or maybe he just didn't bring it to school today."

"That's just it," Amy replied sharply. "He does have a backpack, and he did bring it to school today. I saw it a couple hours ago. It must still be upstairs!"

"Maybe he forgot it by mistake."

"Or maybe he forgot it on purpose because he's got the batting glove in there. Come on, Chase, I have a strong feeling about this. We need to investigate Dave next."

"Well, OK," I said, finally giving in to Amy. "We'll focus on Dave, but if we find out it's not him, then we're going right to Jessica, and you're not going to talk me out of it."

"Fine," she said.

Luckily for Amy, she wouldn't need to hug Dave because his clothes didn't have any pockets where he could hide the glove. She and I also wouldn't need to check the inside of his desk because the back table he was using didn't have any storage space under the desktop.

We could go right for his backpack.

We just needed to figure out a way to get Dave to bring it downstairs. After we thought for a few minutes, I decided just to stand up and go talk to my teacher. When I approached her desk, she put down her paperwork and looked up at me.

"Mrs. Kennedy," I said, "do you trust me?"

"Of course I do. Why do you ask?" Mrs. Kennedy knew something was wrong. I had been down in the dumps since I came back from PE, and I guess my teacher could sense it.

"I need Dave Morrison to bring his backpack downstairs. The other kids from Mrs. O'Connor's class already did, but he didn't. Amy and I think he has something in there that doesn't belong to him."

A look of surprise appeared on Mrs. Kennedy's face. She paused for a few seconds and then started nodding her head. "Chase, I know you're not a tattletale, and I can tell by your tone that you must have a good reason for seeking my help. OK, I'll take care of it."

"Thanks, but there's one more thing. Could you please wait a little while before you talk to Dave? If you call him up right now, he'll probably figure out that you and I were just talking about him. I don't want it to be so obvious."

"Sure, I'll call him up in a couple minutes."

"Thanks, Mrs. Kennedy."

Just as she promised, Mrs. Kennedy waited a bit before asking Dave to come see her.

"Dave," she said, "it's almost lunch time, and I need you to bring down your backpack from upstairs. Your classroom is going to be locked up for the rest of the day, and we need everything out of there."

Dave hesitated.

"Is there a problem?" Mrs. Kennedy asked.

Dave looked like he was trying to think of something to say, but nothing came out of his mouth.

"Dave, is there some reason you don't want to bring your backpack into this room?" she asked a little more firmly.

"Uh...uh, no, ma'am. I'll go get it."

Dave shot me a look on his way out the door.

I figured it would take only a minute or two for Dave to grab his backpack and return to the room, but after five minutes, there was still no sign of him.

"Boy, he's sure taking his sweet time with this," I whispered to Amy.

Just as she was about to respond, Dave walked inside holding his backpack tightly to his chest.

Mrs. Kennedy was becoming quite suspicious by this point and asked Dave to bring the backpack over to her desk.

"Dave, I'd like you to open your backpack," she said.

"I don't want to," he replied.

The rest of the class grew very interested in this conversation and looked up from their books to see what was going on.

Mrs. Kennedy was beginning to lose her patience, but she managed to stay calm and asked once again for him to open the backpack.

"There's something in here I don't want people to see," he admitted quietly.

"Come on, show me, dear," Mrs. Kennedy said, trying to encourage him. "You don't have to worry about anything."

"I really don't want to do it."

This time Mrs. Kennedy wasn't going to take no for an answer. "Dave Morrison," she said sternly, "open this backpack right now!"

Dave was learning what the rest of the kids in this class had learned a long time ago—you don't say no to Mrs. Kennedy.

Reluctantly, Dave grabbed the top of his backpack and slowly started to unzip the main pocket. Inside was a small, white piece of clothing. From where I was sitting, I thought it very well could have been my batting glove. As Dave continued to pull the material out of the pocket, I realized, much to my disappointment, it was far too big to be the glove.

Mrs. Kennedy then grabbed the cloth and began to unfold it. "Why, it's a T-shirt. Dave, this is very nice. Why are you so worried about having people see this?"

Then, she opened it all the way.

None of us could believe what we saw.

It turned out that Dave's T-shirt had a big shovel on the front, and right under it were the words *I Dig Gardening*. Mrs. Kennedy showed the shirt to everybody, and Dave hid his red face in his hands as the other kids laughed.

Mrs. Kennedy tried to comfort him.

"Dave, there's no reason to be embarrassed. Gardening is a great activity for both boys and girls, and I think it's wonderful that you enjoy it so much and that you're a part of the Gardening Angels."

Mrs. Kennedy kept trying to make Dave feel better, but it was no use. He was still embarrassed that everyone just found out that he really did like gardening.

Lunch was now only a few seconds away. As funny as Dave's T-shirt was, I knew I had to keep my mind on my investigation. Last time, when I searched for the cello, Coach Turner took me off campus during lunch, and I wasn't able to talk to any of my friends or teachers. Today, though, I would be right here at school the whole time without any distractions getting in my way.

I was determined to get to the bottom of this mess once and for all.

12:07 p.m.

CHAPTER 13

12:08 p.m.

"**C**hase!" my teacher yelled as I was almost out the door on my way to lunch.

"Yes, Mrs. Kennedy?"

"I forgot the attendance sheet again. Could you please take it down to the office for me?"

"Sure."

"Thanks," she said as she handed me the pink paper.

As I walked down the hall to the office, I began to feel a little sorry for myself. This day wasn't turning out the way I expected. With the semifinal baseball game set for this afternoon, I thought it was going to be one of the best days of the year. So far, though, it had been one of the worst.

My lucky batting glove had been stolen, my best friend had gone home sick, and my time was running out. Less than three hours from now, I would be on the bus to Walnut Grove—with or without the glove. I didn't even want to think about playing the game without that glove.

Soon, I arrived at the office, walked into the entryway, and looked to my left. Suddenly, I remembered what happened the last time I took the attendance sheet to the office. It was something I wish I could forget—looking at the display case and discovering that the cello was missing. I froze and felt a knot in my stomach. The pain and agony of that day came rushing back. Today, I realized, was shaping up to be just like that day.

I heard the voices of two women in the office. Wendy Marshall's mom was there to pay her daughter's cafeteria bill. She was standing at the counter talking to Mrs. Gonzales as I dropped the attendance sheet into a wooden box. Wendy's mom noticed me, and the two of us nodded hello to each other.

"Thank you for your help, Mrs. Gonzales," Wendy's mom said as I turned to leave the office.

"It's my pleasure."

"Again, I'm sorry it took me so long to come in and take care of Wendy's account. I've just been so busy lately."

"It's no problem at all," said the office manager.

"You have a great day."

"You, too, Mrs. Roberts."

Hearing Mrs. Gonzales call Wendy's mom *Mrs. Roberts* stopped me dead in my tracks.

I knew that Wendy Marshall's parents had recently gotten a divorce, and I figured that must be why the girl and her mother had different last names. But still, there was something about the name *Roberts* that rang a bell with me. I just wasn't sure what it was.

I know I've heard that name before, I thought to myself. *Why does it sound so familiar?*

12:16 p.m.

CHAPTER 14

12:17 p.m.

I ate lunch alone. Jenny was home sick, Amy was with the rest of the Gardening Angels preparing for today's tomato showing preview, and I didn't feel like sitting with any of my other friends. I needed some time to myself to try to figure out why the name *Roberts* sounded so familiar.

As I sat on the bench thinking, I felt someone coming up from behind.

It was Brock Fuller.

"Hey, Fan, what's up?" Brock was the only kid at school who still called me by that name. If you ask me, he did it to hold onto the idea that he was still the team's star and I was still a weak player, both of which were clearly no longer the case.

"Hey, Brock, what's going on?" I asked, trying to sound relaxed. It wasn't working. Brock could tell I was still scared of him.

"Take it easy, Fan. I didn't come here to start any trouble. We're teammates now. You don't have to worry. We're on the same side."

Since this morning, I had considered Brock one of my main suspects, but something just occurred to me. Maybe Brock didn't do it. After all, the search of his pockets, desk, and backpack turned up nothing. Also, as much as Brock wanted to be the team's star once again, I didn't think he would hurt his own chances of winning the championship by taking his teammate's glove. I knew how competitive Brock was at everything. Brock Fuller absolutely hated to lose.

Just then, a completely different idea entered my mind. Maybe Brock was up to something. He could be pretending to be nice to me while also being the thief. I quickly ruled out that possibility, though; no offense, I didn't think Brock was bright enough to pull off something like that. Plus, I didn't think any kid could do something so rotten.

Instead, I returned to my first thought—that Brock was innocent. If that were true, Brock could have come over to the bench not to give me a hard time, but because he needed me. In order to win the semifinal game, Brock needed me on the team and needed me to have a good game today.

If I was right about that, I thought it was pretty cool that someone who almost put me through a wall seven weeks ago now *needed* me. Before I could spend any time enjoying that idea, however, Brock started talking again.

"Hey, Fan. I noticed you've been down in the dumps since PE. Usually, you're all dorky and happy. What's going on?"

I had made up my mind. I decided to trust Brock and tell him about the stolen batting glove. Yes, it was risky, but I felt I had to do it. I needed to talk to someone right now, and Jenny and Amy weren't around.

"Brock, you're right. I have been upset since PE. Nobody besides Amy knows this, but someone took my batting glove after practice, and I need to get it back before we get on the bus for the game."

When Brock heard this, he had a look in his eye that I had never seen before and couldn't figure out.

"Dude," Brock declared, "I'll help you find it."

Again, I wasn't sure if I could trust Brock, and even if I could, I didn't know how much help he would be.

"Oh, I don't know if that's such a good idea, Brock," I responded.

"Come on, dude, since your little girlfriend went home sick, you need me. We're teammates. That glove is just as important to me as it is to you, and I'm going to help you find it whether you like it or not!"

"Well, OK," I said, accepting Brock's offer. What else could I do? I knew better than anyone that you don't say no to Brock Fuller.

Brock was getting excited about his chance to be a detective when something suddenly struck me, and I disappeared into my own little world. I closed my eyes and dropped my chin to my chest, the way I often did when I needed to do some deep thinking.

Brock wasn't sure what was happening.

"Dude, are you OK? Hello, dude, are you in there? Is anybody home?"

Just then, it hit me!

"I've got it!" I yelled. "Now I know why the name *Roberts* sounds so familiar."

"Dude, what are you talking about?"

"Mrs. Roberts is Wendy's mother," I continued, ignoring Brock's question. "Brock, who are we playing today?"

"Walnut Grove."

"Right! And who's their best player?"

"Jason Roberts."

"Yes, that's it!"

"What?"

"Wendy Marshall's cousin is Jason Roberts!"

12:45 p.m.

CHAPTER 15

12:46 p.m.

"**I**'m going to go talk to Wendy Marshall right now," I said, feeling confident about the connection I had just made between Wendy's mom's last name and Walnut Grove's star player.

It suddenly made sense why Wendy had been telling me all morning that I would never be as good at baseball as her cousin. She wasn't talking about her second grade cousin, Ryan; she was talking about her other cousin, Jason Roberts.

Even though Wendy went to school at Apple Valley, it was possible that she was rooting for her cousin's team in today's game and stole the batting glove so Walnut Grove would have a better chance to win.

Brock wasn't quite as quick to catch on to all this, so I had to explain it a couple times to him, slowly.

"Oh, I get it now," Brock exclaimed.

"Good," I said. "Now why don't you stay here while I go talk to Wendy."

"Hold on, dude, I'll do it. You stay here. I'll go."

"What? Brock, are you sure you even know how to investigate?" I asked.

"Dude, you're talking to Brock Fuller. Of course, I know how to invetiskate."

"I think you mean *investigate*."

"Yeah, dude, whatever."

"What investigation strategy are you going to use?"

"What?" Brock said impatiently.

"W-h-a-t i-n-v-e-s-t-i-g-a-t-i-o-n s-t-r-a-t-e-g-y a-r-e y-o-u g-o-i-n-g t-o u-s-e?" I repeated.

"Investigation what?" Brock said, shaking his head. "Look, dude, your questions are starting to bother me, and you're making this too complicated. I know you're a master detective and all, but just chill out. I don't need any fancy detective stuff. I know what I'm doing."

Brock started to walk away, but I wanted to give it one last try. "Wait, Brock! I appreciate your help. I really do. But I should be the one to find out from Wendy if she took my glove."

Suddenly, Brock stopped and turned back toward me. The two of us were standing face-to-face, well almost face-to-face. Brock had me by a good six inches and at least twenty-five pounds.

"Look, Fan," Brock said, with both the volume and the anger rising in his voice, "if someone steals a little cello, I don't really care. But, when someone has the nerve to take your batting glove, then it's almost like you're taking something from *me*. Trust me. That's not something you want to do."

I gulped and took a step backward. I was about to say one more thing, but I decided it was no use. Brock's mind was made up, and there was nothing I could do to change it. I let him go.

"At least he's on my side this time," I said to myself when Brock was out of sight.

I could do nothing except sit and wait while Brock was off doing who-knows-what to Wendy Marshall. A bunch of thoughts started racing through my head.

A minute later I looked in the direction of the garden and saw all the girls, and Dave, and Mrs. Simmons gathered around one of the tomato plants. There appeared to be something going on, but from where I was sitting, I couldn't tell what all the excitement was about. I decided to get a closer look, but just as I stood up, I noticed someone coming my way.

It was Brock Fuller.

"Well, any luck?" I asked, wondering what, if anything, Brock had accomplished.

"She didn't do it," Brock announced.

"What? Are you sure? You were gone only a few minutes."

"She didn't do it."

"How do you know?"

"Dude, don't worry about it. Sometimes, the less you know, the better. Trust me. She didn't do it."

I had no idea what had just occurred and was horrified thinking about Wendy's condition at the moment, but I accepted my teammate's declaration. I was grateful that Brock had gone to the trouble of getting this information for me.

More than anything, though, I was freaked out.

12:54 p.m.

CHAPTER 16

12:55 p.m.

Wendy Marshall did not look good standing in line after the bell rang. I was still wondering what happened between her and Brock a few minutes earlier. She didn't have a scratch anywhere, and I didn't think Brock had actually hurt her physically. But the long brown hair that she usually wore in a ponytail was now standing straight up, and her face looked as if she had just seen a ghost. At that moment, if someone asked Wendy her name, I'm not sure if she'd have been able to give the right answer.

It appeared that rookie detective Brock Fuller had invented a brand new investigation strategy: scare the living daylights out of your suspect until you get the information you need.

Once inside, I sat down with Amy to get her caught up with everything that had happened since the beginning of lunch.

"I learned some important things a little while ago, but I couldn't tell you about them because you were over in the garden the whole time."

"Cool. What did you find out?" she replied.

"First, I ran into Wendy Marshall's mom in the office and figured out there's a connection between Wendy and Jason Roberts, Walnut Grove's star player. They're cousins."

"Whoa!" Amy responded. "Are you thinking that she might have taken your glove to help her cousin's team win the game today?"

"Exactly."

"Well then, you should definitely investigate her next."

"Actually, we already did."

"*We?*"

"Yeah, that's the other thing I wanted to tell you. Brock started helping me, and he found out she didn't do it."

"Brock?" Amy asked with a skeptical voice.

"Yeah, Brock."

She took a look over at Wendy and gasped at the sight of her vertical hair and expressionless face.

"Chase," Amy said, "I don't think it's a good idea for Brock to be helping you find your glove. I don't think you can trust him."

"I thought that, too," I replied, "but he's being really nice and helpful to me. At first, I wondered whether he was just pretending to be nice to me while actually being the real thief, but then I figured he wasn't bright enough to pull that off. No offense, he's not the sharpest tool in the shed."

"Yeah, I know, and I agree. And even if he could pull it off, who would do something that rotten, that two-faced? I mean, pretending to work with you while really working against you? No, he wouldn't do that."

"Exactly."

"Still, Chase, think about it. He's been helpful to you for what, an hour? That doesn't mean you should get too close with him."

I then did something I had never done before; I defended Brock Fuller.

"Amy, I disagree. I think I can trust Brock. After all, the two of us are on the same side this time. If I have to play without my glove, and we lose, then Brock gets hurt as much as I do. Think about it."

"I *am* thinking about it," she fired back, "probably not how you want me to be thinking about it, but I'm thinking about it. And what exactly do you mean when you say that you and Brock are on the same side? Are you saying that you, as a member of the baseball team, and I, as a member of the Gardening Angels, *aren't* on the same side?"

"That's not what I meant," I said, trying to calm things down. "Could you please just let it go?"

"Fine," she sighed. "Let's get back to business."

"Cool. As far as I'm concerned, Wendy, Brock, and Dave can all be ruled out as suspects at this point, leaving Jessica as the last remaining possibility. It's time to focus on her."

"Oh, I really don't think she took your glove, Chase."

"Amy, it's pretty clear to me now that Jessica did it. I have good evidence against her, and I've explained it to you. It's almost like you're trying to protect her," I said firmly. "She did it, Amy. She did it."

"Stop saying that!" Amy replied, raising her voice and beginning to lose her temper. "She didn't do it! Stop accusing her! False accusations can really hurt people! Don't you understand how false accusations can hurt people?"

I was stunned by Amy's strong reaction. I had never seen her that upset before. I truly thought there was convincing evidence against Jessica, but I couldn't ignore

Amy's emotional defense of her friend. At this point, I also felt I could trust Brock. Before I could do any more thinking, however, Mrs. Kennedy signaled that it was time for science.

I didn't know what to believe.

1:01 p.m.

CHAPTER 17

1:02 p.m.

Our class loved science. Mrs. Kennedy was always coming up with cool projects for us to do. We didn't just read about science or talk about science. We *did* science. We built, poured, weighed, measured, experimented, and questioned. Her supply closet contained enough chemicals, machines, tools, and equipment to keep any young scientist going for months. Science with Mrs. Kennedy wasn't just a subject. It was an experience.

"Before we begin our science lesson," she announced, "I need to change some of the groups I made because we have so many kids absent today and because a few of Mrs. O'Connor's students are joining us. I need to be sure that each of our visitors is paired with someone from this class so that everyone knows how to carry out our procedures correctly. I want everybody to get off to a great start."

All of us grew curious about the new groupings.

"Amy," Mrs. Kennedy said, looking around the room and tapping her finger to her chin, "why don't you...why don't you work with Jessica."

The two girls smiled at each other from their desks, and Amy started clapping softly to herself. This might have been the first good thing to happen to Jessica all day.

"Dave, you'll work with Chase. I know you two will just *dig* working with each other," Mrs. Kennedy said, unable to control her laughter. "I'm sorry, Dave. I really am. I know I shouldn't be making jokes about your shirt, but I couldn't resist."

Dave and I just stared at each other with blank expressions on our faces.

Mrs. Kennedy kept rearranging the groups until only two students remained.

"Wendy, that leaves only one person. You'll be with Brock."

Immediately, Wendy's eyes became as big as doorknobs, and she froze.

"Wendy? Wendy, dear? Are you OK?" Mrs. Kennedy asked, sensing that something was wrong.

No answer.

"Wendy? Hmm, I wonder what could be wrong with her," Mrs. Kennedy said, looking at Brock.

"Why, dude, I have no idea!" Brock said, acting completely puzzled by Wendy's reaction.

I sat at my desk shaking my head at Brock. I didn't know what was more surprising, the fact that he had just lied to Mrs. Kennedy or that he called her *dude*.

By now, everyone had heard about what happened at lunch with Wendy and Brock. We all sat quietly looking at poor, frozen Wendy until Jessica said, "Mrs. Kennedy, maybe you could give Wendy another partner."

"That's a good idea, Jessica," Mrs. Kennedy replied, "but next time, please try to mind your own business, like Chase does."

Jessica rolled her eyes and let out a frustrated groan. "Ugh!"

"OK, OK, what should we do? What should we do?" Mrs. Kennedy sang to herself, not paying any attention to Jessica. "I know. Chase, I'm going to put you with Brock. Wendy, you'll be with Dave."

Mrs. Kennedy then summoned Wendy over to her desk and quietly asked, "Will that be better, dear?"

"Yes, thank you," Wendy said, catching her breath. The color was beginning to return to her face.

When we were all sitting next to our new partners, Mrs. Kennedy gave the directions for today's experiment. Just as we were set to begin, she made one last announcement.

"I want to remind everyone once again about the importance of safety. As I always say, safety first! You're going to be working with two chemicals today, and if you mix them correctly, everything will be fine."

She then paused for a moment, held up the chemical bottles for everyone to see, and pointed to a safety warning on both the labels.

"But," she continued, "if you're not careful, you could wind up with a mixture that's potentially very dangerous. In fact, the chemical you might create is so dangerous that it's illegal in this state. Sometimes, though, you'll find it in certain substances that are used to make plants grow bigger. If you touch this chemical, your fingernails will turn black, black spots will appear on your skin, and you will experience severe flu symptoms within the next 24 hours."

We all looked around at one another, blown away by Mrs. Kennedy's warning. My teacher could tell she had made her point, but she decided to add one last comment.

"As you know, we've had enough kids going home with the fever lately, so please be careful mixing your chemicals. We wouldn't want anything bad happening to any of you."

1:10 p.m.

CHAPTER 18

1:11 p.m.

"**P**hew!" I sighed after Brock and I finished mixing the chemicals correctly.

"Dude, I was never worried," Brock said. "I've always been great with checimals."

"I think you mean *chemicals*," I corrected.

"Yeah, dude, whatever."

I looked around the room, and it appeared that all the pairs had taken Mrs. Kennedy's warning seriously and mixed the chemicals carefully.

When she saw that everyone had finished the first part of the experiment, Mrs. Kennedy signaled for attention. "Class, for the rest of this activity, your pair will join another pair to make a group of four. Within your group of four, everyone will rotate and have the chance to work with each of the other three members."

Immediately, I was hoping that Mrs. Kennedy would put my group with Amy and Jessica so I could continue my investigation. Fortunately, a moment later, that's exactly what the teacher did, and the two girls did not look happy about it. Still, the four of us moved our chairs together and began working.

For the first rotation I worked with Brock while Amy remained with Jessica. Quietly, I told him that I thought Jessica took the glove and Amy was protecting her.

"Dude," Brock replied, licking his lips and rubbing his hand around his fist. "Just let me take care of Jessica. I'll handle this. I'll handle this."

"Whoa! Down, boy! Down, boy! Easy there, big fella!" I said, remembering what happened to Wendy the last time Brock tried to help. "We'll figure something else out. I promise."

Across the table Amy and Jessica were having their own private conversation. It looked intense. Unfortunately, I couldn't hear what they were saying.

A few minutes later, Mrs. Kennedy's signal told us it was time to change partners and move to the next part of the activity. Amy sat down right next to Brock, who immediately backed away and started blushing.

Several feet away I pulled my chair next to Jessica's and used the direct approach on her, the same way I had used it on Amy when I searched for the cello. The direct approach was an investigation strategy where the detective came right out and accused the suspect of committing the crime. Usually, according to the shows I watched on television, suspects are so surprised by this tactic that they end up confessing their crimes.

"Jessica, earlier today someone took my batting glove, and I think you did it."

The surprised reaction I was hoping to get from Jessica never came. Apparently, Amy had just warned her about everything, and Jessica was ready for me.

"Chase, I did not take your glove."

"I think you did."

"You can think whatever you want, but I'm telling you, I didn't steal your glove."

"Jessica, you can keep denying it, but I have good evidence that it was you, and sooner or later I'm going to find my glove. I think you did it."

Mrs. Kennedy gave us the signal to rotate to our next partner, but Jessica and I weren't done with our conversation.

"I think you did it. I think you did it," Jessica mocked. "Is that all you can say? Is it?"

"No," I coolly replied. "Actually, I have one more thing to say to you."

"What's that?"

"Have fun working with Brock."

As Jessica gulped, I got up and moved next to Amy. She didn't even wait for me to sit down before telling me how betrayed she felt because I now trusted Brock more than her. I told her that I just wanted to keep this about business.

"Amy, I don't want to hurt anyone's feelings. I just want to find my glove. That's it. I'm not trying to make this personal."

"Well, Chase, you are making it personal, and I can tell you this. Jessica didn't take your glove."

I didn't believe that. Amy wasn't turning out to be as helpful as I thought she'd be.

A few feet away, Brock was whispering something in Jessica's ear. He was doing a good job of covering his face with his hand and talking quietly. As a result, Amy and I couldn't see his expression or hear the words coming out of his mouth. We could, however, see the panic in Jessica's eyes and hear her gasping. Obviously, Brock was employing his scare-the-living-daylights-out-of-your-suspect strategy.

For the final part of the science activity, we returned to our original partners. Jessica was freaking out, and Amy was trying to console her. I sat down next to Brock and started to think about where Jessica might be hiding the glove.

"She's too smart to leave it in her desk or her backpack," I reasoned. "So it's got to be somewhere else."

"Dude, where do you think it is?"

"Where else has she been today?" I asked myself. I then closed my eyes, went through the day's schedule in my mind, and thought of all the places on campus she'd been.

Then it hit me!

"I think I know where it is!" I blurted.

"Where, dude?"

"The glove has to be in the gardening shed!"

1:50 p.m.

CHAPTER 19

1:51 p.m.

I couldn't keep my mind on the science journal entry I was supposed to be writing. I needed to find a way to get to the gardening shed—the sooner, the better.

"I have to get into that shed," I whispered to Brock.

"Dude, you should go find Kenny and get a key from him. He likes you. He'd give it to you."

"That's a good idea, but I already thought of that. It won't work because Kenny's home sick, and there's no substitute custodian today."

"Aren't there any other keys you could borrow?"

"There's a master key that opens every lock in the school."

"That's awesome!" Brock replied. "Get that one."

"There's one problem. The gardening shed wasn't built that long ago, and Amy told me it came with a special lock from a different company. The master key won't work on that lock. Only Mrs. Simmons and Ms. Fletcher have the new key. And Mrs. Simmons isn't going to give it to me."

"Dude, then you have to go to Ms. Fletcher."

I knew Brock was right. Though I had already gone up to my teacher once today to ask for a favor, I decided to take a chance and do it a second time.

"Mrs. Kennedy, I'm sorry to bother you again," I said, approaching her chair. "There's something I need to ask you."

"What is it?"

"May I have permission to go down to the office and talk to Ms. Fletcher for a minute? I'll be back as soon as I can."

"Chase, I trust that you have a good reason for making this request. So, I'll let you go."

"Thanks, Mrs. Kennedy. I appreciate it."

When I arrived at the office, Ms. Fletcher was headed the other way.

"Oh, Chase, it's you," she said.

"May I ask you a question?"

"Hold on a minute. There's something I need to take care of. I'll be right back," she said, hustling away.

"Wait! I just wanted to ask you if I could borrow the—"

But it was no use. She was gone.

I took a seat on the bench inside the office and waited. One minute turned into five, and I was getting antsy. Glancing at my watch, I realized that only about an hour remained before the end of school. *I wonder why she's keeping me waiting so long*, I thought to myself.

Just then, I saw her coming back into the office and was relieved.

"Ms. Fletcher, I really need to talk to you."

"That's fine, Chase, but I'm not quite ready for you yet. I just need a few more minutes. In the meantime there's something really important I need from you. I need you to deliver the three boxes of finger paint over in the corner to Mrs. Colby's kindergarten room."

This errand didn't sound that important to me, but before I could say anything to Ms. Fletcher, she disappeared once again down the hall.

I tried to grab all three boxes at once, but it was no use. They were way too heavy. I had no choice but to take one box at a time and make three trips.

Mrs. Colby had been my kindergarten teacher, and she smiled when I entered the room. She stopped her lesson and said, "Children, I'd like you to meet one of my former students. This is Chase."

Some of the kids started laughing when they heard my name, and two boys began repeating it over and over as they chased each other around the room.

"Timmy, Johnny, you boys stop that right now and come back to the rug!" Mrs. Colby snapped. "Now, Chase, what can we do for you?"

"Ms. Fletcher just sent me in here to deliver some boxes. I'll be right back with the other two."

"That's fine, Chase. It's good to see you."

"You, too."

I left the room thinking about how much easier life was in kindergarten. I was about to head back to the office for the next box when something in the distance caught my attention. Ms. Fletcher was standing by the gardening shed talking to Mrs. Simmons. I didn't know what the ladies were discussing, but when I returned to Mrs. Colby's room with the second box, they were still talking.

By the time I delivered the final package, both women were gone. I thought Ms. Fletcher would be heading back to her office, so I hustled to meet her there. Luckily, I arrived exactly when she did, and Ms. Fletcher invited me inside.

"Now, Chase, thanks for your patience, and thanks for helping me with the paints. What can I do for you?"

I was feeling stressed because my time was running out, but I tried to stay calm. "Ms. Fletcher, may I please borrow your key to the gardening shed?"

"I'm afraid that's impossible," she replied.

"Please, it's extremely important."

"A-choo!" went Ms. Fletcher.

"Bless you."

"Thanks. Chase, I'm sure *you* think it's important, but students are simply not allowed in the gardening shed without the approval of an administrator."

"But that's why I'm here, to get the approval of an administrator."

"Oh, but I can't let you go to the shed by yourself."

That gave me an idea.

"Maybe we can walk to the shed together and you can supervise me."

"A-choo! I'm sorry, that's out of the question."

I couldn't tell whether Ms. Fletcher was merely following the rules or whether something else might be going on. I wasn't ready to give up just yet.

"Last time, Mrs. Kennedy gave me the key to the security room."

"But, Chase, you have to understand something. Mrs. Kennedy is not an administrator. Let me make this very clear to you. Only an administrator can authorize you to go inside the shed. I am the only administrator on campus, and I'm saying no."

I tried to think of something else to say, but my mind drew a blank. Ms. Fletcher wasn't going to give me her key, and that was that.

I had been denied.

As I left her office, I felt a tickle in my nose.

"A-choo."

2:15 p.m.

CHAPTER 20

2:16 p.m.

Mrs. Kennedy was reading aloud to the class when I returned from my frustrating meeting with Ms. Fletcher. I found a seat on the back of the rug next to Brock and quietly told him how she wouldn't give me a key to the gardening shed and made it very clear that only an administrator could authorize me to go in there.

Brock started rubbing his hand around his fist and licking his lips. "Dude, I'll take care of her. Just let me take care of her!"

"Whoa, easy there, big fella," I whispered, trying to calm him down. If I wasn't going to let Brock take care of Jessica after seeing what he did to Wendy, there was no way I was going to let him anywhere near Ms. Fletcher. Quickly, I tried to change the subject.

"Say, where is everybody?" I asked, noticing several kids missing.

"Oh, Dave and the other girls were called down to the garden early to get ready for the tomato showing preview."

I felt another tickle in my nose. "A-choo! A-choo!"

Just then, the phone rang. It rang a couple more times before I remembered that I was taking Jenny's turn as Student of the Week and hustled to answer it.

"Hello, student speaking," I panted.

"Hi, it's Mrs. Gonzales from the office. Could you please tell Mrs. Kennedy that Ms. Fletcher has just gone home sick?"

"What? Really? OK."

I hung up the phone and went to give my teacher the message. As she thanked me, I think she could tell that things hadn't gone the way I wanted with Ms. Fletcher.

I returned to my spot on the rug and started analyzing the news I just received from the office. Right away I grew suspicious. I remembered that Ms. Fletcher did sneeze a few times while we were talking, but it didn't seem that serious. *Was she really sick*, I wondered, *or was this merely an excuse to leave campus?*

In addition, I recalled the conversation Ms. Fletcher had with Mrs. Simmons by the shed. *Could there be something going on between the two women? And, if Ms. Fletcher had the glove, was she going to take it with her?*

I began to panic a little bit. Last time, when I determined that Mr. Andrews had stolen the cello, I could find some comfort in the fact that since the principal hadn't left school all day, the cello had to be somewhere on campus. Now, with Ms. Fletcher going home sick, I could find no such comfort. Soon, I figured, that batting glove could be anywhere. I started to panic a little more.

"A-choo!" I went again.

Before I could do any more thinking, though, the phone rang again. This time, I picked it up after the first ring.

"Hello, student speaking."

"Hi, it's Mrs. Gonzales. I'm sorry for calling again, but I forgot to tell you something before."

"What's that?"

"With Ms. Fletcher gone, Mrs. Kennedy has been put in charge of the school as acting principal because she has the most seniority of any teacher on campus."

"The most sen-what?" I asked, confused.

"The most seniority," Mrs. Gonzales explained. "That means she has been at Apple Valley longer than any other teacher. Because of that, she becomes acting principal when the principal and assistant principal aren't here."

"Oh, I get it. Thanks, Mrs. Gonzales. I'll tell Mrs. Kennedy right away."

My teacher took the news from the office in stride. She explained to the class that this had happened two or three times before in her career. It was no big deal.

I found my spot on the rug next to Brock and tried to pay attention to the story Mrs. Kennedy was reading, but I was distracted by some thoughts brewing in my head. I couldn't quite figure out what they meant, so I attempted to sort through them. With my eyes closed, I continued to think, but still no luck.

All of a sudden, it hit me!

Being put in charge of the school may not have been a big deal to my teacher, but it was a very big deal to me.

Mrs. Kennedy was now an administrator!

2:22 p.m.

CHAPTER 21

2:23 p.m.

Having figured out that Mrs. Kennedy, as acting administrator, now had the authority to get me into the gardening shed, I didn't miss a beat. I popped right up to her chair and asked for permission to use Ms. Fletcher's shed key, which, a moment ago, had been delivered to the classroom on her key ring. Mrs. Kennedy didn't say a word. She handed me the key, and I was gone in a flash.

From the garden Mrs. Simmons noticed me approaching the shed.

She didn't seem happy to see me.

For one thing, I was a member of the baseball team whose success was putting her garden in jeopardy. There was also a chance she knew I accused her daughter of stealing the cello seven weeks ago. Alice definitely wouldn't have taken that news well.

"Hi, Mrs. Simmons, I have the approval of an administrator to check something in the shed," I said.

Alice didn't appear eager to let me inside, but she had no power to stop me.

"Fine, dear, you go right ahead," she said, trying to sound gracious. "Oh, I just remembered that I have to go take care of something. I'll be right back."

As Mrs. Simmons stood up and walked away, I headed toward the shed, which was located a good twenty yards from the garden. Grabbing the lock, I felt the eyes of Dave Morrison and the rest of the Gardening Angels on me. With sweat running down their faces and their yellow gardening gloves digging into the dirt, most of them probably had no idea what I was doing there. Jessica and Amy, however, knew full well why I was there, and the two girls gave each other a look.

I opened the lock and stepped inside the shed. There were three shelves on each wall, and I checked everywhere—every nook, every cranny.

The batting glove was nowhere to be found.

The one thing that did catch my attention was a big bag of fertilizer sitting on the ground near the shed door. The safety warning that was on the chemical bottles during science was also on the top of the bag. Even more interesting, I noticed that the fertilizer contained the illegal chemical Mrs. Kennedy mentioned earlier, the one that's sometimes used to make plants grow bigger but that's dangerous to humans.

Could Mrs. Simmons be using this illegal fertilizer to win the tomato showing? I wondered. *I knew she wanted to win, but I never thought she'd cheat.*

The shock of discovering the fertilizer was soon overpowered by the disappointment of not finding my batting glove anywhere inside.

Amy saw me exiting the shed. She came up to me and touched my hand.

"Are you looking for your batting glove?" she asked softly.

"Yes. I checked all over, but it's not in there."

"Are you sure?"

"Yeah, I'm sure."

"Go in again and look in the way back corner on the floor," she told me.

"What? Why? There's no point."

"Just look back there."

"Why? Are you hiding something from me?"

"OK," Amy sighed. She sighed again, and it seemed as if she wanted to get something off her chest. Before saying a word, though, she took a look behind her to make sure nobody was listening to our conversation.

She stepped closer to me and said, "It's just that...I saw...I saw...no, I can't do this...I can't."

"Can't what?"

"I can't do this to a friend of mine."

"Amy, what are you talking about? Just tell me already, and it will be all over."

"OK, fine. You were right about me protecting Jessica," she admitted.

"I was?"

"Yes, I saw her in the back corner of the shed earlier. She was hiding your batting glove."

"Are you sure?"

"Yes."

"Wow, thanks," I said. "I know that wasn't easy for you, but you did the right thing."

"It doesn't feel like it."

"I know, but you did."

"Anyway, I have to get back to the garden. Good luck finding your glove."

"Thanks, Amy."

As she walked away, I just stood there for a minute admiring her honesty and courage. I watched her find a spot next to the other Angels over in the garden and then decided the time was right to head to the corner of the shed and find my lucky batting glove once and for all.

I knelt down and felt around for the glove. All of a sudden, I heard the door slam behind me! I ran to the door and tried to open it, but it was no use.

I was locked in.

2:30 p.m.

CHAPTER 22

2:31 p.m.

Several questions flooded my mind when I realized I was locked inside the gardening shed: *How am I going to get out? How much time is it going to take before I can escape from here?* And, most important, *who did this to me?*

As I tried to calm myself, I overheard people arguing right outside the shed door. The conversation sounded heated. Due to the thickness of the walls, however, I couldn't identify the voices or determine what they were saying. I was pretty sure that one of the voices belonged to Alice Simmons, but beyond that, I didn't know. She could have been talking to one or more people, and they could have been kids or adults.

I pressed my ear to the shed door so I could hear better. One of the voices was definitely Alice's, and she seemed to be speaking with one other girl.

"What? You've got to be kidding!" Mrs. Simmons said in disgust to whomever was standing next to her. "That is absolutely out of the question, young lady! I can't keep him locked in there. I'm opening the door this instant. Now back away!"

The voices died down. Alice jangled her keys for a little while trying to find the right one, and then I could hear the shed door being unlocked. A few seconds later, the door opened. Alice was the only person standing near the shed when I walked outside. All the Angels were over in the garden.

"My dear, I'm so sorry about the door," Alice said. "Such an unfortunate accident! A burst of hot air must have come out of nowhere and blown the door shut. I rushed over to let you out as soon as I saw what happened."

I didn't believe for a second that this was an accident, and I thought the only burst of hot air in the immediate area right now was coming out of Alice's mouth. Still, I was glad to get out of there. I thanked Mrs. Simmons for opening the door and raced back to class. It seemed as if I'd been in there forever, but luckily, only a few minutes had passed.

Heading to the room, I had to think fast. The tomato showing preview was starting soon, and I figured this event would be my last good chance to catch the thief and get my glove back. I closed my eyes, dropped my chin to my chest, and began to focus my mind on the task at hand.

A minute later I entered the room. The other kids were cleaning up, packing their belongings, and getting ready to leave for the preview. Mrs. Kennedy asked me to help Brock put the science materials back in the supply closet.

"Boys," she warned, "be sure to wear the yellow safety gloves in case any chemicals spilled on the counter earlier. Whatever you do, don't take your gloves off."

For some reason those last few words echoed in my head. "Take your gloves off, take your gloves off."

Then it hit me!

I felt a jolt of energy race through my body, and in a matter of moments, I had a plan.

"Brock, I know what we're going to do!"

Instead of asking about the plan, however, Brock started to panic. "Dude, we're running out of time! We're running out of time!" He was new to these pressure situations.

"Brock, it's OK. I've been through this before."

"No, dude, it's not OK. We're running out of time!"

Though it was kind of fun watching Brock squirm like this, I needed to stay focused on the steps of my plan. I gave him a look of confidence and calmly repeated the words I used a minute earlier.

"I know what we're going to do."

2:39 p.m.

CHAPTER 23

2:40 p.m.

Brock and I stayed behind for a minute while the rest of the class headed down to the garden. We needed to put my plan into action. I explained everything to Brock slowly, but he didn't get it.

I explained the plan again.

"Huh? I don't follow."

I then decided to try a new approach and have Brock repeat everything I said back to me, but he kept making mistakes.

"You want me to make my backpack darker?"

"No," I corrected, "I want you to get a black marker."

"And you want me to take the marker and fry some snails in a pan?"

"No, I want you to take the marker and apply it to your nails and hands."

"But that will turn them black."

"That's the whole point."

"And it will leave marks on my skin!"

"Brock, that's the whole point!"

"Oh, I get it now."

"Good, now go grab a black marker."

Once Brock completed his task, the two of us hustled to catch up with the rest of the class, and I ran straight to my teacher.

"Mrs. Kennedy, you're going to give a little speech right before the showing starts, aren't you? Don't administrators always give introductions before important school events?"

"I hadn't really thought about it," Mrs. Kennedy answered, "but I guess I am."

"When you give your speech, I have a suggestion for you."

"Oh yeah, what's that?"

"Well, I remember what you said during science today. I think you should tell everyone what a great hobby gardening can be, but also mention the importance of using chemicals safely. Why, you could even give the same reminder you gave us earlier. Safety first. Isn't that what you always tell us?"

Mrs. Kennedy seemed pleased that I had taken her safety warning so seriously. Happily, she agreed to use my idea.

What she didn't know, however, was that I had another reason for making this suggestion.

All the pieces were in place. As long as Mrs. Kennedy came through with her speech and Brock came through with his part of the plan, I figured that the whole school would soon know the identity of the person who took my batting glove.

The moment of truth was now at hand.

2:46 p.m.

CHAPTER 24

2:47 p.m.

"**W**hat is she doing back here?" I asked myself when I noticed Ms. Fletcher walking from the teachers' parking lot over to the tomato garden. "I thought she went home sick."

Ms. Fletcher found a spot off to the side, studied the crowd, and started talking to Dave Morrison. "Dave, I think it's wonderful that you're a part of the Gardening Angels. Gardening is such a terrific hobby for both boys and girls."

Dave didn't say a word. Embarrassed, he just stood there, probably wishing that all the ladies at school would stop telling him that.

I was sitting next to Brock a few feet from the garden as the rest of the upper grade classes were getting settled. I was still wondering about Ms. Fletcher, but I had more important things to think about—namely, the two key players in my plan, Mrs. Kennedy and Brock.

I felt confident that my teacher would deliver her speech exactly as she said she would, but I was crossing my fingers and worrying about whether Brock would remember his part. He finally seemed to understand the plan, but would he come through under pressure, when it counted? I couldn't be sure.

With the audience now in place, Mrs. Kennedy welcomed everyone to the showing and began her introductory speech. She followed my suggestion perfectly. At first, she described her own love of gardening and explained that gardening is a fantastic activity for both boys and girls. Immediately, everybody looked at Dave, who hid his face in his hands to shield himself from the attention, the way he did earlier when Mrs. Kennedy exposed his T-shirt.

She then moved to the next part of her speech and began discussing safety.

"Children," Mrs. Kennedy went on, "if you decide to take up gardening, please be careful. Many fertilizers and chemicals are involved in creating a beautiful garden, and you need to handle the materials in the right way."

Those were the words I was waiting for, and I turned to Brock to see if my partner in crime fighting was ready.

Right on cue, Brock came through like a champion. Just as I had instructed, he stood up and began to freak out. He looked at his hands and pretended to be shocked that his skin and fingernails had all turned black.

"Ahh!" he screamed. "My nails! My skin! Dudes, I touched the tomatoes! I touched the tomatoes!"

Instantly, every one of the Gardening Angels who was in Mrs. Kennedy's class during science seemed to remember what she said about what happens to people who touch the illegal chemical that's sometimes used to make plants grow bigger. I'm not sure if they had any idea whether or not Mrs. Simmons ever used that chemical on the tomatoes, but after seeing Brock's reaction, they freaked out as well. Quickly, they all ripped their yellowing gardening gloves off their hands to check their skin and nails.

And there it was!

The batting glove was right there on her hand.

The observers gathered around the garden couldn't believe what they saw.

Coach Turner couldn't believe it.

Mrs. Kennedy couldn't believe it.

Brock Fuller couldn't believe it.

Wendy Marshall couldn't believe it.

Dave Morrison couldn't believe it.

Patty Fletcher couldn't believe it.

Alice Simmons couldn't believe it.

Jessica Kingman couldn't believe it.

The lucky batting glove was on the hand of Amy Simmons.

As happy as I was to see my glove, I was incredibly disappointed in Amy.

"So, it was *you* all along," I said, shaking my head.

Before Amy could answer, Alice stepped in and asked her daughter if this could possibly be true. Turning back and forth between her mother and me, Amy's face looked like a volcano ready to erupt.

"OK, OK, I admit it!" she yelled after hesitating a minute. "It was me! *I* took the glove! *I* did it! None of you have any idea how much pain I've been in these last few weeks. First, Chase, you accuse me of something I didn't do. Nobody accuses me! Nobody! And now, because you've become such a good hitter, the baseball team keeps winning, and my garden may get destroyed! I wasn't going to let that happen! No way! Not under my watch! I couldn't take it anymore! So, at the end of PE, I ran over and took your glove."

Amy then stopped and began to catch her breath. She turned her head to the side and looked as if she was trying to figure something out.

"But, Chase," she asked, "all day long you thought Jessica was your number one suspect. You even said that you didn't think I did it. What changed? How did you know it was me?"

"At first, I did think it was Jessica, and she has been my number one suspect all day. That never changed. But when Mrs. Kennedy told us four kids from your class were coming, and then you showed up as the fifth, I got just a little suspicious. I wondered whether you arranged, for some reason, to get sent to our room. Then, you convinced me to solve this case by myself and not tell an adult. That made me a bit more suspicious. The way you kept pushing Dave and Brock as suspects and the way you talked about what happened last time with the cello also made me suspicious. So, throughout the day I still thought Jessica took my glove, but I never *completely* ruled you out as a suspect."

"And that was it?" Amy asked.

"No," I replied. "All afternoon it seemed that you were protecting Jessica from Brock and me. Then I realized something. Maybe you weren't protecting Jessica; maybe you were protecting yourself."

"And that was it?" Amy asked.

"No," I replied. "The final straw came when I was locked in the shed and heard arguing outside. Somebody wanted to keep me in there. I couldn't tell who it was, and I figured it was either you or Jessica. But it didn't matter."

"What do you mean it didn't matter?"

"When I came up with the plan to have Brock trick your gardening club by pretending to be sick, I thought both of you would take your gloves off. So, whichever of you was wearing my batting glove under your gardening glove, I knew we would trap the real thief."

"Whoa, dude, that's smart," Brock said admiringly. "You didn't tell me any of that."

"I can't tell you all my secrets, Brock. You're already a better baseball player than I am. I can't let you become a better detective, too."

Brock smiled.

I was happy to build up my teammate, and I could tell that Brock really appreciated getting complimented for something other than being a great athlete. He wasn't used to hearing praise about his mind, but he had just come through for me in a big way, and I felt Brock deserved those kind words. I then turned away from Brock and focused my attention back on Amy.

"And to think, you almost got away with it."

"Yeah," Amy responded, pointing angrily at me, "and I would have gotten even with you once and for all!"

I ignored her outburst and calmly turned toward Ms. Fletcher, who was standing nearby.

I looked at the acting principal and said, "Ms. Fletcher, take her away."

As the administrator walked with Amy and her mom down to the office, all the guys on the baseball team gathered around me and touched the lucky batting glove that was now back on my hand. A few even talked to it.

Coach Turner stepped up to us and said, "Come on, boys. Time to get on the bus. We got a game to win."

3:00 p.m.

Epilogue

ater that afternoon Apple Valley Elementary defeated
Walnut Grove, 9 - 8, despite four home runs by legendary
slugger Jason Roberts. The victory in the semifinals came in
the last inning on another of my game-winning hits.

Two days later, the hiring committee selected Patty
Fletcher to be the new principal. It turned out that she got
her dream job without any help from Alice Simmons, who
resigned from the committee after her daughter Amy was
expelled from school.

With her new authority as principal, Ms. Fletcher was
quickly able to change the schedule Mr. Andrews had created
and find another field for our team's upcoming championship game.

As a result, there was no need to level the garden, and the
Angels went on to win the Annual Tomato Showing. Before

declaring Apple Valley's garden the winner, however, the judges tested the tomatoes and found out that Alice Simmons had never used any illegal chemicals. The Gardening Angels won fair and square.

The championship baseball game was another nail-biter, and my single in the last inning knocked in the winning run. I was even named the Most Valuable Player of the tournament.

Coach Turner asked me to represent the team at the special trophy presentation held right after the game. As I stood on the little stage waiting for Mr. Green, the person in charge of the league, to hand me the award, I couldn't stop staring at it.

The trophy was a real beauty. Standing about two feet high, it had a golden statue of a batter at the top, and the baseball diamond in the middle looked like it was made from real diamonds.

"Son, your name is Chase, right?" Mr. Green asked at the start of the ceremony.

"Yes, sir."

"I understand you've been a busy young man these past few weeks."

"Yes, I guess I have," I agreed, though I never really thought about it like that before.

"You found an important cello and helped save your school's music program?"

"Yes."

"And you even got to keep the cello. Am I right?"

"Yes."

"And today, you got the hit that won the game and the league championship for your school?"

"Yes."

"Well, son, let me tell you something."

Wait a minute, I thought to myself, *was I going to get to keep the trophy like I got to keep the cello? That couldn't be possible, could it?*

"Today, it is my pleasure to present this magnificent trophy to Apple Valley Elementary," Mr. Green said, handing it to me.

"Wow, thank you, sir."

"You bet, Chase. And do you know where it's going?"

"No, sir," I replied, even though there was a chance I did.

"Usually, all the sports trophies in our league are kept in the coaches' offices. This one, however, is so special, it will not be kept in Coach Turner's office. It will be kept someplace else."

I couldn't take any more of this. My insides were going crazy with anticipation.

"I'll ask you again, Chase. Do you know where this trophy is going?"

"No, sir, where?" I said, barely able to speak at this point.

"This trophy will be kept...in a special display case in the entryway that leads into your school's office."

I have to admit, it would have been cool to keep the trophy, but I realized that wouldn't have been right. It had to be displayed somewhere where the whole school could see it. I just smiled and lifted it high overhead as my cheering teammates carried me off the field. On the bus ride back to school, I held the trophy and cradled it like a baby the entire way home.

About the Author

Steve Reifman is a National Board Certified Teacher, author, and speaker living in Santa Monica, California. *Chase for Home*, the second installment in the Chase Manning Mystery Series, is the sequel to the award-winning *Chase Against Time*. Be on the lookout for the next Chase Manning mystery, *Chase Under Pressure*.

Steve has also written several resource books for teachers and parents, including *Changing Kids' Lives One Quote at a Time*, *Rock It!*, and *Eight Essentials for Empowered Teaching and Learning, K–8*. You can find teaching tips, blog posts, and other valuable resources and strategies for teaching the whole child at www.stevereifman.com. You can follow Steve on Twitter at www.twitter.com/stevereifman.

72261683R00090

Made in the USA
Lexington, KY
28 November 2017